Smart ABOUT Safety

Emergency—Call 911

by **Teddy Slater**   illustrated by **Anthony Lewis**

Scholastic Inc.

**New York Toronto London Auckland
Sydney Mexico City New Delhi Hong Kong**

For the Margulies brothers — Fred and Paul —
who'd never tease each other!
—T.S.

ISBN 978-0-545-24601-9

12 11 10 9 8 7 6 5 4 3 2 1   10 11 12 13 14 15/0

Printed in the U.S.A.   40

First printing, September 2010

Jack knew just what to do in case of an emergency.

"Call 911," his mother had told him.

"Call 911," his father had told him.

And his teacher had told Jack's whole class the same thing.

So when his dog chewed his homework, Jack picked up the phone and began to dial.

"Who are you calling?" Jack's mother asked.

"I'm calling 911," Jack said. "My homework is ruined."

"Oh, Jack," his mother said. "That's not an emergency. An emergency is when something really dangerous happens.

"A fire is an emergency," Jack's mom explained. "A flood is an emergency. If someone suddenly gets very sick or hurt — that's an emergency. You should only call 911 when you need special help right away."

Jack hung up the phone and sat down at the table with his mom.

"Wally learned that lesson the hard way," Jack's mom said. "Wally was a brave little lamb. He wasn't afraid of anything.

"But Wally's brother Woolly was afraid of everything — especially wolves. Wally loved his brother, but he also loved to tease him.

"One windy day, Wally and Woolly went to the meadow to munch on some grass. A cool breeze shook the bushes at the edge of the meadow.

"'Help!' Wally cried. 'There's a wolf in those bushes.'
Woolly saw the shaking bushes and ran for home.
'Come back, Woolly!' Wally called. 'I was only kidding.'

"The next day was even windier. Wally and Woolly were playing in the meadow when the wind began to howl. 'Help!' Wally cried. 'I hear a wolf in the bushes.'

"Woolly heard the howling sound and ran for home. 'Come back, Woolly!' Wally called. 'I was only kidding.' But Wally kept running.

"After a while, Wally headed home, too. It was no fun playing alone.
Halfway home, he heard soft footsteps behind him. He turned
around, and there it was . . . a real live wolf!

"Wally ran as fast as he could, crying, 'Help, Woolly! Help! A wolf is chasing me!'

Woolly heard his brother's cries. But this time he didn't believe there really was a wolf. He'd been fooled before."

"Oh, no!" said Jack.

"Oh, yes!" said his mom. "Wally made it home just in time. Woolly slammed the barn door behind him, and the wolf went away. After that, Wally never teased his brother again. And he never called for help unless it was really an emergency."

SAFETY TIPS

Dial 911 when you need help
for an emergency.

Speak clearly to the person who
answers the call. Tell him or her
your name, your address, and
what the emergency is.

Never dial 911 unless
it's a real emergency.